Safari Countdown:
One, Two, Three!

By: Brett Neal

In the bright sunshine, underneath a blue—green tree, began our counting safari — won't you count with me?

"One" said the monkey, swinging high on a vine, his smile as bright as the sunshine.

"Two" roared the lions, twin brothers Leo and Lou, their manes all tawny and thickly strewn.

"Three" trumpeted the elephants, lined up by the river, their trunks raised high, making the leaves shiver.

"Four" chattered the zebras, with stripes black and white, prancing around in sheer delight.

"Five" hissed the snakes, in the tall, swaying grass,
watching all the animals pass.

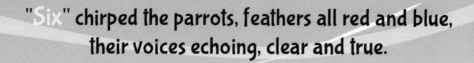

"Six" chirped the parrots, feathers all red and blue,
their voices echoing, clear and true.

"Seven" rumbled the hippos, in the cool, muddy pool,
looking oh–so–sleepy, as they begin to drool.

"Eight" honked the geese, flying in the sky, their for—
mation like a ribbon up high.

"   " barked the hyenas, laughing all the while, each with a distinct, mischievous style.

"Ten" growled the cheetahs, swift and fleet, their spots like golden treasure, oh so sweet.

With a hop, a leap, a swing, and a twirl, we've counted to ten in our safari world!

From one to ten, what a delightful spree, counting safari animals, under the blue-green tree!

Remember these numbers, remember them well. For the next adventure, only time will tell!

1. How many monkeys did you spot?

2. What number comes after the zebras and before the lions?

3. Can you name three animals you saw in the safari?

4. Which animal was the fifth one you counted?

5. Were there more hippos or elephants in our counting adventure?

6. What sound does the animal on the seventh page make?

7. Which animal had the longest arms on our safari?

8. How many animals did we count in total on our safari journey?

9. Did you see any birds during our counting safari? If yes, which one?

10. Which was your favorite animal to count, and why?